MARTHA WALKS THE DOG

Susan Meddaugh

Walter Lorraine (wr) Books

Houghton Mifflin Company Boston

For Martha

Walter Lorraine ⟨wl⟩ Books

Copyright © 1998 by Susan Meddaugh

www.houghtonmifflinbooks.com

Library of Congress Cataloging-in-Publication Data

Meddaugh, Susan.
    Martha walks the dog / written and illustrated by Susan Meddaugh.
        p.   cm.
    Summary: Martha the talking dog rescues the neighborhood from a
bully dog with the help of a parrot.
    RNF ISBN 0-395-90494-3   PA ISBN 0-618-38005-1
    [1. Dogs—Fiction. 2. Bullies—Fiction.] I. Title.
PZ7.M51273Maq 1998
[E]—dc21   97-47172
                                                                   CIP
                                                                    AC

Printed in Singapore
TWP 10 9 8 7 6 5 4

Martha's family had a wonderful party trick.
They knew that when they said:

Martha would.

Guests were always amazed.

Martha learned to speak the day she ate alphabet soup.
The letters went up to her brain instead of down to her stomach.

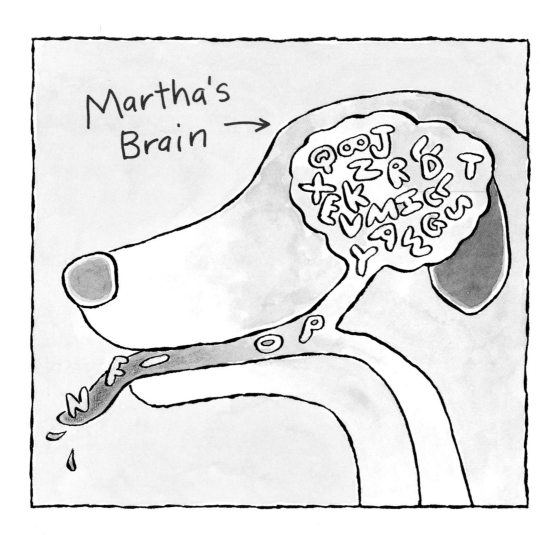

Martha's family was so proud.

But Martha never let flattery go to her head.

Martha loved her daily walks.
As usual her pals were scratching,
sniffing, or snoozing, and Cisco
was chasing Nelson the cat.

But there was one difference. A house down the street had
been sold, the FOR SALE sign replaced by a new sign.

Martha went to investigate.

She was puzzled. She didn't see a dog.

Suddenly a mountain of fur burst from under the porch stairs,
lunging and growling at Martha.

Before she could say a word,
a man came out of the house.

BAD DOG BOB!
BAD DOG!!

Bad Dog Bob retreated
to chew on his chain.

As the weeks passed, Martha hoped that Bob would calm down.
But every time Bob saw Martha he charged to the end of his chain
and barked ferociously at her.

It wasn't just Martha.
Bob barked at anything that moved.

BAD DOG
BOB!
BAD
DOG!

His owner was just as ferocious.
On Martha's daily neighborhood rounds
she always tried to ignore their angry
barking and yelling.

One day on her walk
Martha heard a nicer voice.

"Thank you," she said. "What's your name?"
"Thank you," said the parrot.
"What's your name?"
"My name is Martha," said Martha.
"My name is Martha," said the parrot.
"Hmmm," thought Martha.

Then Martha had an idea.

Martha had to stop the lesson when two people came into the room.

"Words are such fun," thought Martha.
She turned around just in time to see Cisco chase Nelson the cat into Bob's yard.

In a flash Nelson was through the yard and over the fence.

Cisco was a manly poodle, but he was no match for Bob.
Martha spoke up immediately.

18

She unleashed a torrent of words as Cisco made his escape.

Bob walked slowly toward her, but Martha wasn't worried.
She knew he would soon reach the end of his chain.
But when Bob came to the edge of his yard he kept on walking.

when I say...

uh oh.

sit!   STAY!

"Can we talk?" asked Martha.
Bob opened his mouth . . .

and Martha ran for her life.

OOF!!

Round and round Bob chased Martha.

Nothing she yelled
had any effect on him.

Martha was running out of words and breath.

Finally she could run no more.
She closed her eyes and prepared to die.

And then she heard a voice from above.

GOOD DOG!

Martha opened her eyes.

She couldn't believe what she saw.

BOB WAS SMILING.

"Great dog!" said Martha.
"Great dog!" said the parrot.
Bob's hackles went down.

Bob's tail began to wag.

Just then Bob's owner came running up.
Martha sank back into the bushes.

"Don't yell," Martha whispered.
"Don't yell," said the parrot.
"Be nice," Martha whispered.
"Be nice," said the parrot.

"It's a miracle!" said Bob's owner.

"Good dog, Bob," he said. He didn't yell.

"Looks like the beginning of a beautiful friendship," thought Martha. And she continued to walk the dog.